Note to parents, carers and teachers

Read it yourself is a series of modern stories, favourite characters and traditional tales written in a simple way for children who are learning to read. The books can be read independently or as part of a guided reading session.

Each book is carefully structured to include many high-frequency words vital for first reading. The sentences on each page are supported closely by pictures to help with understanding, and to offer lively details to talk about.

The books are graded into four levels that progressively introduce wider vocabulary and longer stories as a reader's ability and confidence grows.

Ideas for use

- Begin by looking through the book and talking about the pictures. Has your child heard this story before?

- Help your child with any words he does not know, either by helping him to sound them out or supplying them yourself.

- Developing readers can be concentrating so hard on the words that they sometimes don't fully grasp the meaning of what they're reading. Answering the puzzle questions on pages 30 and 31 will help with understanding.

For more information and advice on Read it yourself and book banding, visit **www.ladybird.com/readityourself**

Book
Band
7

Level 2 is ideal for children who have received some reading instruction and can read short, simple sentences with help.

Special features:

Frequent repetition of main story words and phrases

Short, simple sentences

Large, clear type

Careful match between story and pictures

Sly Fox picked up his big, black bag.

"I'm going to catch Red Hen and eat her," he said.

10

11

"I will catch you," said Sly Fox, and he ran round and round and round.

16

17

Educational Consultant: Geraldine Taylor
Book Banding Consultant: Kate Ruttle

A catalogue record for this book is available from the British Library

Published by Ladybird Books Ltd
80 Strand, London, WC2R ORL
A Penguin Company

003

ISBN: 978-0-72329-369-9

Printed in China

Sly Fox
and Red Hen

Illustrated by Diana Mayo

Red Hen lived in a little house in a tree.

Sly Fox lived in the wood.
And he was hungry.

Sly Fox picked up
his big, black bag.

"I'm going to catch
Red Hen and eat her,"
he said.

Sly Fox hid in Red Hen's little house.

"I'm the fox, I'm the fox, I'm really sly. You can't beat me, however you try!" said Sly Fox.

13

Red Hen saw Sly Fox and jumped up out of his way.

"You're the fox, you're the fox, you're really sly. But you won't catch me, however you try!" said Red Hen.

"I will catch you," said
Sly Fox, and he ran
round and round
and round.

Red Hen's head went
round and round, too.
She fell down into
Sly Fox's big, black bag.

Sly Fox ran into the wood.
The big, black bag was
heavy and Sly Fox sat
down to rest. Then he
fell asleep.

Red Hen jumped out of
the bag.

"You're the fox, you're
the fox, you're really sly.
But you won't catch me,
however you try!" said
Red Hen.

23

Red Hen put some
heavy stones in the bag.
Then she ran all the
way home.

Sly Fox tipped the bag into the cooking pot.

"I'm the fox, I'm the fox, I'm really sly. I will eat you. Say goodbye!"

The stones fell SPLASH!
into the cooking pot.

"Oh no!" said Sly Fox.
"I did not catch Red Hen!"

How much do you remember about the story of Sly Fox and Red Hen? Answer these questions and find out!

- **Where does Red Hen live?**

- **Where does Sly Fox live?**

- **How does Sly Fox catch Red Hen?**

- **What does Red Hen put in the bag?**

Look at the pictures and match them to the story words.

Red Hen

Sly Fox

stones

bag

wood

Read it yourself with Ladybird

Tick the books you've read!

For beginner readers who can read short, simple sentences with help.

Level 2

Beauty and the Beast ☐
Chicken Licken ☐

Little Red Riding Hood ☐
Nature Trail ☐
Sports Day ☐
Pirate School ☐
Rumpelstiltskin ☐
Sleeping Beauty ☐
The Gingerbread Man ☐

Sly Fox and Red Hen ☐
The Tale of Jemima Puddle-Duck ☐
The Three Little Pigs ☐
Why Lion Roarrrrs! ☐
Topsy and Tim: The Big Race ☐
Town Mouse and Country Mouse ☐
Dom's Dragon ☐

For more confident readers who can read simple stories with help.

Level 3

YOU won't like this present as much as I DO! ☐
The Elves and the Shoemaker ☐

Hansel and Gretel ☐
Harry and the Bucketful of Dinosaurs ☐
Jack and the Beanstalk ☐
Furi on Music Island ☐
Poppet Stows Away ☐
Rapunzel ☐
The Red Knight ☐

 Available on the **App Store**

The Read it yourself with Ladybird app is now available for iPad, iPhone and iPod touch

App also available on Android devices

LC
J

RULERS AND THEIR TIMES

LOUIS XVI, MARIE-ANTOINETTE
and the French Revolution

by Nancy Plain

BENCHMARK BOOKS

MARSHALL CAVENDISH
NEW YORK

For my mother, who also loves history

ACKNOWLEDGMENTS

With thanks to Paul B. Cheney of the Department of History, Columbia University, New York City, for his expert reading of the manuscript.

And special thanks to Miriam Greenblatt, who developed the concept for the Rulers and Their Times series.

Benchmark Books
Marshall Cavendish Corporation
99 White Plains Road
Tarrytown, New York 10591-9001
Website: www.marshallcavendish.com

Library of Congress Cataloging-in-Publication Data
Plain, Nancy.
Louis XVI, Marie Antoinette and the French Revolution / by Nancy Plain.
p.cm — (Rulers and their times)
Includes bibliographical references and index.
ISBN 0-7614-1029-5 (lib. bdg.)
1. Louis XVI, King of France, 1754–1793—Juvenile literature. 2. Marie Antoinette, Queen, consort of Louis XVI, King of France, 1755–1793—Juvenile literature. 3. France—History—Revolution, 1789–1799—Juvenile literature. 4. France—Kings and rulers—Death—Juvenile literature. [1. Louis XVI, King of France, 1754–1793. 2. Marie Antoinette, Queen, consort of Louis XVI, King of France, 1755–1793. 3. Kings, queens, rulers, etc. 4. France—History—Revolution, 1789-1799.] I. Title. II. Series.
DC137 .P55   2001   944'.035'0922—dc21   [B]   00-057152

Printed in Hong Kong
3 5 6 4 2

Picture Research by Linda Sykes Picture Research, Hilton Head SC
Front cover: (left) Schoenbrunn Palace, Vienna/Erich Lessing/Art Resource, (right) Réunion des Musées Nationaux/Art Resource NY; page 3: Laurie Platt Winfrey, Inc; pages 8–9: Musee Carnavalet/AKG London; page 11: Giraudon/Art Resource NY; page 11: Hofberg, Vienna/AKG London; page 12: Pushkin Museum/AKG London; page 15: The Art Archive, London; page18: Muse des Beaux-Arts, Lyon, France/Giraudon/Art Resource; page19: Musee Bonnat, Bayonee, France/ Bridgeman Art Library; pages 20, 37, 68: Private Collection/Bridgeman Art Library; page 23: Versailles/Superstock; page 24 Versailles/Giraudon/Art Resource; page 26, 50: Réunion des Musées Nationaux/Art Resource; page 27 Prado, Madrid/Bridgeman Art Library: pages 28, 33, 36, 40–41, 46; page 30: Musee Carnavalet, Paris/AKG London; page 31: Explorer, Paris/ Superstock; page 48: AKG, London; page 54: Giraudon/Art Resource; page 55: Glasgow University Art Gallery, Scotland/Bridgeman Art Library; pages 56, 60: Musee Carnavalet, Paris/Dagli Orti/ The Art Archive; page 62: Louvre/Superstock; page 66: Musee Carnavalet, Paris/Giraudon/Art Resource; page 68: Louvre, Paris/Giraudon/Art Resource; page 72: Uffizi/Giraudon/Art Resource; page 64–65: National Gallery, London/Bridgeman Art Library

Contents

"Long Live the King!"

In 1775 King Louis XVI rode to his coronation in a coach pulled by horses harnessed in silver and gold. Soldiers of the royal cavalry and sixteen more magnificent coaches accompanied him to the great cathedral in Rheims, France. There, in the glow of stained-glass windows and the light of crystal chandeliers, the ancient, jeweled crown of the French kings was placed on his head. Louis was a member of the Bourbon dynasty, which had been founded in 1589. Like the Bourbon kings before him, he would rule by "divine right," the belief that he had been put on the throne "by the grace of God." After the ceremony, Louis touched the heads of two thousand sick people, who hoped that his sacred power would heal them. Then he and Queen Marie-Antoinette walked among the crowds, who cried with joy and shouted, "Long live the king!"

France, the largest country in western Europe, was also one of the wealthiest and most powerful. Even stronger than its army was its cultural influence. Monarchs and nobles throughout Europe often spoke elegant French instead of their native languages. They imitated French architecture, read French literature, collected French art. And there was nothing on the Continent to compare with the splendor of the palace of the French kings at Versailles.

Along with the grandeur and prestige, Louis XVI had inherited serious problems. The previous king, Louis XV, had involved the country in the Seven Years' War, a war so costly that much of

Louis XVI is shown with the emblems of royalty—the scepter, the crown, and the white plumes of the Bourbon kings. Louis was a weak but kindhearted king, who even during the Revolution tried hard not to cause bloodshed among his people.

France's wealth had to be used to pay for it. In addition the French people were deeply divided. A small number of nobles were enormously rich, while millions of peasants lived on the brink of poverty and hunger. In between the two extremes was a rapidly growing middle class. As its members achieved economic success, they wanted to share status and power with the nobles.

It was an age when tradition clashed with new ideas. France in the 1700s was the center of a movement called the Enlightenment. Its philosophers constantly questioned authority and encouraged people to think for themselves. They believed that knowledge and reason could be used to create a better world. The brilliant writer Voltaire called for an end to injustice, superstition, and religious intolerance. Another famous philosopher, Jean-Jacques Rousseau, imagined a society in which freedom and equality would be achieved through the basic goodness of human nature.

During the reign of Louis XVI, economic problems and Enlightenment ideas combined to inspire people from every group in society to demand change.

But on his joyous coronation day, Louis did not know that, in time, the peoples' cheers would turn to shouts of hatred. He did not know that in 1789, the hurricane of the French Revolution would tear through the country, sweeping away the old regime and destroying him and his family in its blast.

PART ONE

On the last night of Louis XVI's life, his family bade him good-bye in the Temple prison. As he prepared himself for death, Louis's greatest fear was for his family. His daughter, Madame Royale—on her knees before her father—was the only one in this little group who would survive the Revolution.

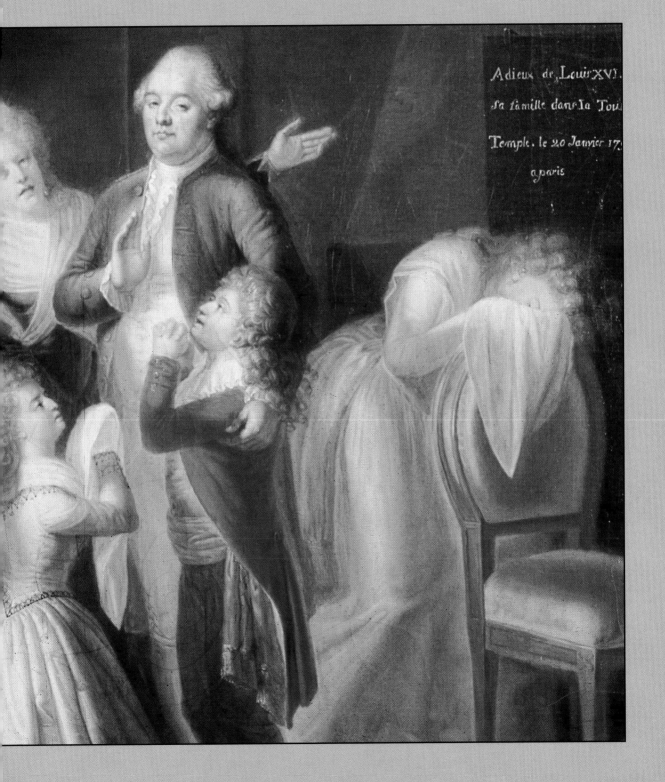

Adieux de Louis XVI
sa famille dans la Tou
Temple. le 20 Janvier 17
a paris

An Arranged Marriage

Marie-Antoinette, the little Austrian archduchess with reddish blond hair, was only fourteen when she married Louis-Auguste, the dauphin, or future king of France. She had met her fifteen-year-old husband just two days before the wedding. Their marriage, at first, had nothing to do with love. It had been arranged by Marie-Antoinette's mother, Maria Theresa, Empress of the Holy Roman Empire, and Louis-Auguste's grandfather, King Louis XV of France. Austria and France, longtime enemies, had only become allies a few years before, in 1756, to fight Prussia and England in the Seven Years' War. The union of the two young people was meant to strengthen this shaky political bond. Their wedding, on May 16, 1770, with fireworks and feasting and guests blazing with diamonds, was one of the most dazzling occasions ever celebrated at Versailles.

It is hard to imagine two people more different from each other than Marie-Antoinette and Louis-Auguste.

Antoinette, as she was usually called, was a member of Austria's Habsburg dynasty. She was born in Vienna, on November 2, 1755, the youngest of the empress's sixteen children. Antoinette's beloved father, Emperor Francis I, died when she was only nine. With her delicate features, blue eyes, and bright curls, she was

Marie-Antoinette developed a love for music early in life. Growing up in the Habsburg palaces of Austria, she was known for her spirited liveliness, but could carry herself, when she wanted to, with regal poise.

often described as radiantly beautiful. Her personality was sparkling as well. She loved to laugh and play and was adept at getting her own way. Before her marriage a French tutor came to Austria to turn Antoinette into a proper Frenchwoman. He found her to be sweet natured and intelligent, skilled at playing the harp and clavichord, but uneducated in almost every other way. "A little laziness and much frivolity [silliness] make it very difficult for me to teach the Archduchess," he complained.

Unlike his future wife, the young Louis-Auguste was well educated, competent in such subjects as physics, foreign languages, math, and even mapmaking. He was also deeply religious, and as dauphin, he gave much thought to the responsibilities he would have as king.

Louis-Auguste had none of his wife's charm. He was shy, over-weight, and clumsy. According to one noblewoman, "He looked like some peasant shambling along beside his plough." He had no interest in the glamorous social life at Versailles. And perhaps because he knew that the courtiers made fun of him, he could often be rude. But he had an unusually kind heart and a strong sense of morality. He planned one day to be a good king.

Born in 1754 Louis-Auguste was orphaned at the age of twelve, when his mother, Marie-Josèphe, died of tuberculosis. Both his elder brother and his father, the son of Louis XV, had died earlier of the same disease. Louis-Auguste had little in common with his four younger siblings, so he sought relief from his loneliness in books. He also loved physical labor, spending hours on carpentry and wood carving and making iron locks in his special forge. He was happiest, however, galloping at top speed through the forests beyond Versailles, hunting deer and wild boar.

Distrustful of his Austrian wife at first, Louis-Auguste left Antoinette, newly titled "dauphine," to adjust to the French court by herself. She had a hard time of it. In contrast to the relaxed atmosphere of the palaces of her childhood, every aspect of life at Versailles was hemmed in by strict rules of etiquette. Courtiers were required to attend formal ceremonies every day. And there was almost no privacy. Antoinette was usually surrounded by a crowd of nobles, even while her hair and makeup were being done. A special lady-in-waiting was assigned to guide her, and Antoinette nicknamed her "Madame Etiquette."

On May 10, 1774, King Louis XV died of smallpox. The courtiers immediately rushed to find the new king and queen. Louis-Auguste and Marie-Antoinette were on their knees praying together and crying, "Oh God, oh God, protect us. We are too young to reign!"

Louis-Auguste was crowned the next year and took the name Louis XVI. His grandfather had begun his own reign known as the "Well-Beloved." But because of scandals and wasteful spending, Louis XV had died truly hated by the people. Louis XVI vowed to be different. He would use his power for the good of France. As Marie-Antoinette wrote, he had the "greatest desire to make people happy."

A Country Divided

Who were the French people? Since the Middle Ages they had been divided into three separate orders, or estates. By tradition and law, each estate had its own status and its own role to play in French society.

The clergy, or members of the Catholic Church, were known as the first estate. They were powerful because their religion was the official religion of France. To have any legal rights, a French person had to be a Catholic. Every country village had its ancient church, where a local priest conducted services. In the larger towns there were towering cathedrals, the architectural wonders of France. In these grand churches high-ranking clergy, such as cardinals and bishops, were in charge.

The clergy saw themselves as keepers of the public welfare. They ran schools, hospitals, and shelters for the poor. But they were also living in an intolerant age, and cruel things were done in the name of religion. During the reign of Louis XV, officials in one province arrested a nineteen-year-old nobleman for antireligious writings. He was sentenced to have his tongue cut out and to be burned at the stake. (This case, and others like it, prompted Enlightenment writers to fiercely criticize the Catholic Church.)

The nobles, or aristocrats, were the second estate. They were the socially elite of France. Some could trace their noble titles back for centuries, to the time when feudal lords ruled their lands like

The French described the three estates this way: The nobles were "those who fought," the clergy were "those who prayed," and the people in the third estate were "those who worked." This drawing, done at the start of the Revolution, shows the worker carrying the whole country on his shoulders.

private kingdoms. They were called "nobles of the sword." Others acquired their titles when they paid for the privilege to hold high government office. These administrators, lawyers, and judges were called "nobles of the robe."

The wealthiest nobles of both types left their turreted castles in the countryside to live with the king at Versailles. In exchange for their loyalty, Louis XVI gave them apartments in the palace, pensions, and many other gifts. He appointed noblemen to all the highest government jobs. They became generals, ambassadors, and ministers in the king's Grand Council. And they participated eagerly in the glittering court life at Versailles. Louis ran the palace according to the customs of his ancestor, Louis XIV, who had created there a vast "city of the rich."

Everyone who was neither a member of the clergy nor of the nobility was lumped together in the third estate—and a very diverse group it was.

These "commoners" included the middle class, or bourgeoisie. They were the fastest growing portion of the population. Middle-class men—never women—were doctors, lawyers, bankers, and merchants. Some men of the third estate made fortunes in overseas trade. But unless they could afford to buy noble titles and become nobles of the robe, members of the bourgeoisie could never rise to the highest posts in the government, the military, or even the Church.

It was possible for middle-class families to improve their lives. It was almost impossible for the workers and peasants, those stuck at the bottom of the third estate.

French cities were home to an increasing number of workers trying to earn enough to survive. Some were skilled artisans, or craftsmen—wigmakers, cobblers, bakers, tailors. Those without skills became peddlers or did odd jobs. They lived in crowded, dirty slums.

But France was still mostly a farming country, from the golden wheat fields of the north to the olive groves of the south. Eighty percent of the population were peasants who worked the land. The majority struggled daily just to feed their families. They were sharecroppers who rented tiny plots of land from wealthy landowners and paid for them with a portion of their small harvests. Using farming methods unchanged for centuries, the peasants were, as one eighteenth-century traveler observed, the "mules" of French society.

Bread and Taxes

When Louis XVI became king, France had no written constitution. There were no laws that applied to everyone throughout the land. The legal system was a tangled web. Some of the country's thirty-nine provinces relied on written laws, while others were guided only by a hodgepodge of local customs. Even more confusing, there were areas where several legal districts overlapped. One town had fifty-three local courts!

The country was governed by the king, with his Grand Council of ministers, and thirteen courts, called *parlements*. These were not composed of elected officials who represented the people; only noblemen could serve in them. The *parlements* tried court cases and also "registered," or made official, the king's new laws. The *parlement* of Paris was the leading court, with legal authority over about one-third of France. The *parlements* liked to be seen as "protectors of French liberty" against the tyranny of the Bourbon kings. But their real goal was always to protect the special privileges of the second estate.

"Privilege" was a word that enraged most people in the third estate. They were weighed down by a staggering number of taxes. But because of traditional privileges, the first and second estates paid almost none.

The Church, which owned about one-tenth of the country's land, paid no taxes at all. Instead, Church officials made voluntary

The lives of most French peasants were hard. Years of physical labor and constant worry have left their mark on this woman's face.

donations to the government, known as "free gifts." The nobles, who owned even more land, paid almost nothing. Wealthier members of the third estate also managed to whittle down the amount they paid.

The poorest in France, the peasants, paid the most. They paid the basic tax known as the "taille," or "cut." They paid taxes on salt, soap, and other goods. They paid a tithe, or percentage of their incomes to the Church. To the landowners, the peasants owed rent and many different kinds of dues, following customs from feudal times. Peasants were also required, for no pay, to build and repair the country's roads, a program called the "corvée."

All these taxes were due even in times of bad harvests. A series of these crop shortages began in 1770 and lasted for almost twenty years. Coarse bread made from wheat, barley, or rye made up most of a poor person's diet. So when their daily loaves were scarce or too expensive, peasants and urban workers became frantic. In the worst years they crowded the marketplaces to demonstrate and, often, to riot. And because France's population was steadily growing, the demand for bread became more and more intense.

Louis and Marie-Antoinette knew that taxes and bread shortages were crushing the poor. The king's coronation had almost been postponed because of rioting. Mobs of angry people had looted bakeries and threatened to lynch merchants who were caught hoarding grain. When the rioting was over, two looters were taken to be hanged, shouting, "We die for the people!" The queen—who certainly never said anything like "Let them eat cake"—had wept when she heard about these deaths.

Louis wanted to reduce the tax load of the poor, but his government needed money. France had suffered total defeat in the Seven Years' War (1756–1763), losing to England almost all its colonies in North America. (In American history this war is known as the French and Indian War.) The expenses of war had caused a huge deficit, or debt; the government owed more money than it was

All three estates are shown here bearing the burden of the huge national debt. But it was the king's attempt to raise more taxes to pay that debt that was a major cause of the Revolution.

taking in. Throughout his reign Louis XVI would appoint a series of finance ministers who tried to save France from bankruptcy. But every time they proposed taxing the clergy and the nobility, the Parisian court rebelled. And without the consent of this most powerful court, none of the other *parlements* would agree to the proposals, either.

In theory Louis was an absolute monarch, with the right to pass any law he wanted. But he never had total power. He needed public opinion on his side, and he needed the *parlement* of Paris to *enforce* his laws. When his first finance minister, Robert Turgot, suggested sweeping reforms and an end to tax privileges, the *parlement* of Paris objected bitterly. Louis's greatest fault was weakness. He gave in to the *parlement* and fired Turgot.

The king's next minister was a Swiss banker named Jacques Necker. Instead of taxing the nobles, he borrowed even more money to pay back government loans. France's deficit was soon skyrocketing out of control.

The Monarchy in Trouble

While Louis divided his time between hunting and governing, Marie-Antoinette lived a separate life in the huge palace. As queen, she could now ignore the hated rules of etiquette, and she devoted herself to having fun. "You see, I am so terrified of being bored," she wrote. Antoinette shocked the older courtiers, whom she called the "Centuries," by acting as no French queen ever had before. She dashed around the palace grounds alone in a fast little carriage. She danced all night at masked balls and cheered wildly at the horse races. She gathered around herself a clique of young nobles who gambled away millions at cards—one game lasted thirty-six hours! Separated forever from her Austrian family and friends, she made new, close friends, for whom she often found high-paying court appointments.

The young queen and her "favorites" escaped the boredom of court life at the Petit Trianon, a beautiful pavilion in the park at Versailles. They held dreamlike, candlelit parties on the nearby lake, parties to which the king seldom came. Another delightful hideaway was the Hamlet, a model village and farm. There the queen and her friends played at being milkmaids, using pails made of the finest French porcelain.

Antoinette developed a passion for diamonds and went into

Marie-Antoinette's friendly manner, dazzling beauty, and splendid clothes made her a favorite subject for the painter Élisabeth Vigée-Lebrun. In this portrait, the queen wears the type of high, feathered headdress that was popular at Versailles during her reign.

debt to buy millions of francs worth of these "trifles." She became a trendsetter in fashion. Her dressmaker designed for her almost two hundred outfits a year, from formal gowns embroidered with gold and pearls to simple "country" dresses of striped cotton. The queen and the court ladies competed for the most elaborate hairstyles, having their powdered curls arranged to such heights that they could barely fit into their coaches.

By the age of twenty, Antoinette already had dangerous enemies. A powerful group of court nobles had hated her from the start because she was Austrian. They published terrible lies about her, accusing her of shocking, immoral behavior. Her frivolous pastimes and irresponsible spending only fed more rumors.

In her letters a worried Maria Theresa warned her daughter that she had "lost all sense" and was "heading straight for disaster." And her brother Joseph II, who was coruler of the Holy Roman Empire, called her a "featherhead." In a letter to her, he wrote, "I can only foretell great unhappiness for you. . . ."

This is a view of the lake at the Petit Trianon. Even the king needed an invitation to visit Marie-Antoinette in her private refuge.

But when her first child was born in 1778—a daughter known at court as Madame Royale—the queen slowed down her social life a bit and drew closer to the king. In 1781 the dauphin, heir to the throne, was born. He was followed, in 1785, by another boy, the duke of Normandy.

Antoinette proved to be an excellent mother, but neither she nor Louis could stop the lies swirling around her. "Why should they hate me?" she would ask one day. "What have I ever done to them?"

In 1778 Louis made a decision that would have an earthshaking impact on his reign. He declared war on England and committed the French to fighting in the American Revolution. By helping the Americans, Louis hoped to boost French trade in North America. He also wanted to punish England for defeating France in the Seven Years' War. He got his revenge, especially in 1781, when French troops under General Rochambeau helped Washington's army force the English to surrender at Yorktown.

But the American Revolution aroused the French people's interest in democracy. Parisians were fascinated by Benjamin Franklin, American ambassador to France from late 1776 to 1785. The famous inventor of the lightning rod, with his simple clothes and thrifty ways, spoke of the new American republic, where elected representatives obeyed the will of the people. French officers, such as the marquis de Lafayette, returned from American battlefields as heroes. Copies of the Declaration of Independence were translated into French. It seemed to many that the Americans were putting into practice the ideals of the Enlightenment by creating a government based on tolerance and liberty. Talk of similar change spread throughout France.

Benjamin Franklin became a celebrity at Versailles and in Paris. He won much support for the American Revolution among French nobles, who did not realize at the time that their enthusiasm for democracy would help bring about their own downfall.

Louis *was* trying to make reforms. In the 1780s he ended the corvée in many provinces. He outlawed the use of torture to obtain confessions. He granted more rights to Protestants and Jews, and he allowed more freedom of the press. But faced with a stubborn *parlement* of Paris, it was becoming harder and harder for him to govern.

"Long Live the Nation!"

Taking part in the American Revolution had left France even deeper in debt than before. The royal treasury was almost empty. Louis and a third finance minister tried to impose a tax on all landowners, including clergy and nobles. The *parlement* of Paris called the king a "despot." It claimed that only a special assembly of representatives of all three estates—an Estates General—could approve such a tax. Louis, far from being a despot, backed down. He gave permission for the Estates General to meet. It was a decision he—and the *parlement* of Paris itself—would soon regret.

Delegates from all over France came to Versailles in May 1789. They marched in a grand opening-day parade: the clergy in magnificent robes, the nobles on their finest horses, and the commoners—lawyers, administrators, merchants—dressed in plain black. The king was greeted with cheers, but when the queen rode by, there was dead silence. Four years earlier, she had been falsely accused of secretly plotting to buy a fabulously expensive diamond necklace. Now the people even blamed her for the national debt—"Madame Deficit" they called her—although the expenses of running Versailles were actually only 6 percent of the total budget.

On June 4, the king and queen's eldest son, the seven-year-old dauphin, died of tuberculosis. "My son is dead and nobody seems to care," said Antoinette. The family retreated to another palace to grieve. During the king's absence from Versailles, the French Revolution picked up steam.

The delegates of the third estate, who represented more than 90 percent of the population, took control of the Estates General. By the time Louis returned, they had renamed it the "National Assembly." On June 20 the delegates found their meeting hall locked, so they met instead in an indoor tennis court. There they took the Tennis Court Oath, vowing to stay together until they

The famous artist Jacques-Louis David depicted the dramatic scene in which the delegates of the third estate took the Tennis Court Oath. Once the third estate decided to write a constitution, there was no turning back.

had given France a constitution. The king, after much indecision, agreed to order the first and second estates to join the delegates in the new National Assembly. What had begun as a struggle between the king and the nobles in *parlement* had turned into a revolution of the middle class. Government by special privilege was over.

That year the people were in as much turmoil as the government. There was a shortage of bread. Food prices were the highest of the century. Paris was full of beggars who shook their fists at the carriages of the rich as they rolled by. And throughout France, people were rioting once again. Louis sent troops to Paris to keep the peace. But when the revolutionaries saw the soldiers, they cried, "To arms!"

On July 14 a crowd of workers in search of weapons attacked the Bastille, a medieval prison with walls fifteen feet thick. They freed the seven prisoners inside, and killed the prison's governor. Then they paraded through the streets with his head on a pike. When the king heard about the fall of the Bastille, he exclaimed, "But this is a revolt!" "No, Sire," he was told. "It is a revolution."

France was in chaos. In the countryside peasants seized food supplies and land, burned châteaus, and murdered nobles and officials. Many aristocrats left the country. As Versailles emptied, Antoinette cried. She would have fled, too, but Louis refused to leave. He was determined to save his throne by appearing to cooperate as much as possible with the revolutionaries.

In August the nobles who had remained in the National Assembly gave up their feudal rights as landowners. The clergy surrendered their claim to the tithe. In August, too, the Assembly wrote a statement of the ideals by which it wished to govern: the Declaration of the Rights of Man and Citizen. Strongly influenced

This watercolor was painted at the time of the storming of the Bastille and based on an eyewitness account of the incident. The rebels succeeded in taking over the Parisian prison partly because many French soldiers refused to fire on the crowd.

by America's Declaration of Independence, it held that all men are "born and remain free and equal in rights." It called for political power to be shared by all citizens, and it called for religious freedom, and the rule of law.

Louis waited to sign the August decrees. They did away with all tradition, the "old regime," as it was now being called. While he waited, the Parisians took the Revolution into their own hands.

On October 5, 1789, thousands of women—and some men disguised as women—marched to Versailles, demanding bread. They were armed with pitchforks, guns, and pikes. The marquis de Lafayette, now commander of the citizens' army, the National

Guard, also arrived with two thousand soldiers. The king was now forced to sign the Assembly's decrees, and in doing so, hoped to achieve peace.

But at dawn the next day, a mob of women stormed the palace, looking for the queen. "Death to the Austrian!" they screamed. "We'll wring her neck! We'll tear her heart out!" Antoinette escaped death by running through a secret passageway. With daylight, the mob, aided by the National Guard, forced the royal family to travel with them back to Paris. One hundred deputies of the National Assembly followed. On the road the people shouted, "Long live the nation!" instead of "Long live the king!" Louis, Antoinette, and their two remaining children were now captives of the Revolution. They would never see Versailles again.

In the summer of 1789, a severe shortage of bread caused riots throughout France. In October, about six thousand women marched in the pouring rain from Paris to Versailles to petition the king for bread.

"Liberty, Equality, Fraternity"

Settled in Paris, the National Assembly continued to remake the government. It rejected rule by divine right and disbanded the *parlements*. It replaced the old tax and legal systems. Ignoring the uneven boundaries of the old provinces, it reorganized France into eighty-three "departments." To pay the national debt, it seized all Church land and put it up for sale. And it placed the clergy under government control. This was hardest for Louis to accept because he was deeply religious. But he had little choice. The constitution that the Assembly was writing provided for a king, but one with almost no power.

The royal family was now living in the Tuileries palace. Louis's younger sister, Madame Elisabeth, was with them, too. The king felt he was just a "shadow of royalty" because he had so little to do. The queen, who had once been so frivolous, showed a newfound courage. In their despair Louis and Antoinette grew very close.

They decided to escape from Paris. Their goal was to settle in the town of Montmédy, in the province of Lorraine, on the north-eastern border. There, protected by loyal troops, they would try to regain power. The queen's close friend Count Axel Fersen made the plans. On the night of June 20, 1791, he managed to sneak the family out of the Tuileries. In a green-and-yellow coach, they almost reached safety. But they were recognized and stopped in the town of Varennes. "There is no longer a King in France," said Louis bitterly, as officers of the National Guard forced the family back to Paris. During the long journey, they were spat at and threatened. The attempted escape had further weakened the monarchy.

The Revolution was far from secure. Nobles who had emigrated were trying to persuade other European countries to invade France. Within the country, much of the population thought the revolutionaries had gone too far. And the people were still burdened by the old problems—high prices and a shortage of jobs and bread.

By 1792 members of the Jacobin Club, the most radical group in the Assembly, had taken control. In April the Assembly declared war on Austria, now ruled by Marie-Antoinette's nephew, Emperor Francis II. The revolutionaries hoped to distract the French people from their problems at home and also to spread the Revolution throughout Europe. At first Austrian and Prussian forces easily defeated the French army. As the enemy marched toward Paris, the citizens panicked.

The Jacobin Club, based in Paris, established chapters all over France. The signs held by this crowd say, "Long live the Jacobins," and "Long live Marat." Marat was an extreme radical who was in favor of beheadings to achieve revolutionary goals.

For many, fear turned to hatred. They hated the queen because she was Austrian and because they believed the lies—more vicious than ever before—that were still being printed about her. They hated the king because they suspected that he, too, was on the enemy's side. On August 10 about twenty thousand revolutionaries from all over France attacked the Tuileries palace. The royal family was forced to flee, without even a change of clothes, to the hall where the Assembly was in session. The Assembly imprisoned them in the Temple, a dark fortress from which there was little chance of escape.

The Revolution had entered a new phase. Many of its former leaders, such as Lafayette, had fled the country. The struggle was no longer a revolt of the middle class, most of whose members wanted a constitution *and* a king. Now the people in power—the Jacobins together with the sansculottes, or radical workers of Paris—wanted to do away with the monarchy completely. And they feared that the old regime would return—if France lost the European war.

But, in September, the French defeated the Prussians in a large battle. The Assembly, in a burst of confidence, renamed itself the National Convention. The Convention immediately abolished the monarchy. It adopted the slogan Liberty, Equality, Fraternity. France would now be a republic, governed solely by an elected assembly. But first the revolutionaries needed to be rid of the king.

The Convention had found letters in Louis's correspondence showing that he was secretly against the constitution. He was put on trial and found guilty of "conspiring against liberty" and many other charges. He was sentenced to death.

The Reign of Terror

Louis faced his death, said one witness, with "superhuman courage." On the night of January 20, 1793, he said good-bye to his sobbing family. He made his little son promise never to seek revenge for his death. The next morning he was beheaded on the guillotine. A young guardsman triumphantly held up the dripping head for the people to see. "Long live the Republic!" shouted the crowd, and some rushed forward to taste the former king's blood.

The rest of Europe was afraid that the Revolution would spread. By February France was at war with almost every major European power—England, the Netherlands, and Spain, as well as Austria and Prussia. There was civil war, too. In western France thousands of royalists and pro-Church peasants rose up against the Revolution.

The Convention formed the Committee of Public Safety to guide France through the war and to keep alive the Revolution at home. The committee, led by Jacques Danton and Maximilien Robespierre, enacted radical social reforms. It declared free education for young children and abolished slavery in French colonies overseas. It tried hard to "dechristianize" France, vandalizing churches throughout the land. It even created a new calendar, renaming the months and selecting 1792—the year the monarchy was abolished—as "Year I."

Robespierre, a lawyer, soon became the most powerful man on the Committee of Public Safety. He began to carry out his policy

The shrewd and fanatical Robespierre rose to power by constantly pitting one revolutionary group against another. Although he was the mastermind of the Reign of Terror, he chose to hide behind closed doors as the tumbrils rolled by. Feared by all, he sent many of his closest associates to the guillotine, until he himself was beheaded, in 1794.

of "terror," or constant executions, to crush the enemies of the new Republic. His first victim was Marie-Antoinette.

She was only thirty-seven, but her hair had turned white from suffering. After Louis's death, the revolutionaries had taken her son away from her. "God himself has forsaken me. I no longer dare to pray," she wrote. Then they moved her to a cold, damp cell in another prison, the Conciergerie, which was known as the "waiting room" to the guillotine. Three attempts to rescue her had failed, and her Austrian family did nothing to help. Many outrageously false charges were brought against her during her trial. Only one charge—that she had sent French war plans to the Austrians—was true. Of this the Committee actually had no proof, but the jury understood that its job was to condemn the queen to death.

On the morning of October 16, 1793, only a few hours after her exhausting, two-day trial, Antoinette dressed herself in a white gown and black satin shoes. Louis had been driven to his death in a coach, but she was taken to the guillotine in a tumbril, or rough, wooden cart. An immense crowd turned out to watch as she passed by, pale and still. Like her husband, she kept her perfect dignity and remarkable courage to the end. (Madame Elisabeth was executed in 1794, and the dauphin died in prison in 1795. Only Madame Royale survived.)

The reign of terror spread. Guillotines were wheeled into town squares all over France. About 16,000 people, from every social class, were beheaded: princesses, peasants, nuns, generals, old

Jacques-Louis David made this quick sketch of Marie-Antoinette as she was driven to the guillotine. The once beautiful queen now looked like an old woman. Arriving at the scaffold, she walked quickly up its steps, fulfilling the vow she had made to herself to die bravely.

men, young mothers, children. One woman was beheaded for having cried at her husband's execution. Flags now proclaimed Liberty, Equality, Fraternity, or Death!

But by July 1794 the people had had enough. Royalist uprisings had been crushed, and foreign armies were retreating from French soil. The Convention now turned on Robespierre himself and beheaded him and his followers. The reign of terror was over.

Middle-class moderates returned to the Convention. They closed the Jacobin Club and overpowered the sansculottes. They abolished most of the radical reforms, while trying to keep those from the early phase of the Revolution. Churchs again opened their doors. A new committee, called the Directory, took charge of the government. The Directory was so unstable, though, that in 1799 it would turn to a general named Napoleon Bonaparte for support. But that is another story.

Looking at the Revolution

Louis XVI and Marie-Antoinette were two of the world's unluckiest monarchs. They came to the throne at a time when France's outdated social and political system was long overdue for a change. Perhaps if gentle, indecisive Louis had been a stronger king, he could have guided that change, instead of letting the storm clouds of revolution break over his head. They broke with brutal fury, killing tens of thousands of people and ending a way of life based on centuries of tradition. But while the Revolution shattered France, it also helped to shape the modern world.

The revolutionaries fought for individual liberties, such as freedom of religion and freedom of the press. They fought for political equality among citizens, so that more people would have a voice in the government. Although they did not achieve all of their stated goals (the vote was granted only to men who owned property), they did begin the long process toward a more just society. Even today, over two hundred years later, people still look to the ideals of the French Revolution as they fight to establish democracies around the world.

PART TWO

The lives of French peasants were much the same during the eighteenth century as they had been in the Middle Ages.

The Land

France is almost the largest country in Europe, second only to Russia. It is approximately six hundred miles long and six hundred miles wide, about the size of the states of Colorado and Wyoming together. Except for the northeastern border that it shares with Belgium, France's borders are natural ones. It is surrounded by the Alps and Pyrenees mountains, the Atlantic Ocean and the Mediterranean Sea, and one long river, the Rhine. The climate is generally moderate, but the north of France shares the snow and colder temperatures of northern Europe, while much of the south tends to be warm and dry. It is a country of many different regions, as varied as they are beautiful. In the time of Louis XVI, the regions were further divided into thirty-nine provinces, whose boundaries dated from feudal times.

Northern France is an area of fertile, rolling plains, where peasants in the 1700s grew wheat. It includes a region known as the Île–de-France ("Island of France"). Surrounded by the waters of three great rivers—the Seine, the Oise, and the Marne—the Île-de-France was the center of Louis XVI's kingdom because it contained both Paris and Versailles, only twelve miles apart. Louis owned several wonderful palaces in the region. The countryside around them was thick with forests of beech and oak. These were the royal hunting grounds, the favorite refuges of the Bourbon kings. Amazingly, Louis XVI traveled outside the

Île-de-France only once during his entire reign.

In the northwest are the regions of Normandy and Brittany. Normandy is a land of apple orchards, fields enclosed by high hedges, and steep cliffs along wide beaches. It is on the English Channel coast, so many of its oldest houses are in the English style, white stucco trimmed with dark wood. The coast of Brittany is rugged and windy, dotted with fishing villages. In the time of Louis XVI, the port city of Nantes, in Brittany, was a wealthy commercial center. The French conducted their slave trade through Nantes, exchanging captives from Africa for sugar and coffee from French colonies in the West Indies.

France's longest river, the Loire, flows through several regions, from the center of the country to its western coast. During the Renaissance, kings and nobles built many castles along the Loire. They are among the most magnificent in Europe—fairy-tale towers of pale stone, encircled by moats and set amid gardens and forests.

The Loire River has its source in the region called the Massif-Central, which covers much of south-central France. This mountainous region, with its extinct volcanoes and isolated villages, was very poor in the eighteenth century. Peasants in the Massif-Central herded sheep and grew chestnuts, which sometimes supplied the bulk of their diet.

Provence, in the southeast, is a hot, dry region of terraced farms, olive trees, and houses with red-tiled roofs. Its largest city is Marseilles, which has always been France's major port on the Mediterranean Sea. During the Revolution, the people of Marseilles were among the most radical in the country. From them came the song *The Marseillaise*, which became the theme song of the revolutionary movement.

EUROPE IN THE TIME OF
LOUIS XVI AND MARIE-ANTOINETTE

BALTIC

SEA

PRUSSIA

POLAND

RUSSIAN

EMPIRE

AUSTRIA

IRE Vienna

BLACK

SEA

EAST

OTTOMAN

EMPIRE

A view of Marseilles, the old port city on the Mediterranean Sea, painted in the time of Louis XVI and Marie-Antoinette.

Although France's roads were probably the best in Europe during the eighteenth century, travel was still slow and difficult. So the regions kept their distinct characteristics and, in some ways, were like separate countries. Largely according to their regions, people reacted differently to the Revolution. While the French in many provinces were enthusiastic about it, people in parts of western France fought hard to save the old regime.

Versailles and the Bourbon Kings

Louis XIV, who lived from 1638 to 1715, was the strongest of all the Bourbon kings. The Sun King, as he was called, became a truly "absolute monarch" through his forceful personality and attention to detail. "I am the State," he proudly declared.

His long reign was a golden age for the arts in France. He employed painters, poets, and musicians, and he even danced in his own ballets. Louis XIV believed that great architecture was the perfect symbol of power, so he decided to build the palace of Versailles. It was to be a monument to his glory. He selected the most talented artists of the day to do the work: Le Vau for architecture, Le Brun for painting and decorating, and Le Notre for landscape design. Completed in 1682 Versailles was the grandest palace in Europe, the envy of other monarchs. Until the fall of the old regime, it would be home to the royal court, as well as the center of government in France.

The palace was constructed of brick and pale gray stone in the balanced and orderly classical style. Visitors often got lost inside, because it had one thousand rooms, connected by gleaming marble halls and sweeping staircases. Louis XIV filled Versailles with every imaginable luxury: paintings, tapestries, patterned carpets, furniture of solid silver, golden candlesticks on marble stands.

Versailles was originally only his father's hunting lodge, but Louis XIV made it his lifelong building project. He enlarged it to become the grandest palace in Europe and the place where he consolidated his absolute power.

The most famous room of all was the Hall of Mirrors. Important court receptions were held there. Its high ceiling was painted with heroic scenes of the Sun King's life. Its mirrors reflected the view from seventeen tall windows by day, and at night they glowed from the light of a thousand candles.

The gardens at Versailles were a masterpiece. They were laid out in complex geometric shapes and filled with orange trees and flowers of every color. In the Sun King's time water splashed from fifteen hundred fountains, many of them carved in the shapes of cupids and mermaids. In the palace grounds long pathways lined with trees and statues led to reflecting ponds. And there was even a Grand Canal, where the king's courtiers went boating.

The Sun King commanded France's most prominent nobles to live with him at Versailles. Under his own roof, he knew he could control them and limit their power. To impress them with his magnificence, he turned every aspect of his day into a court ceremony: waking, dressing, going to mass, eating, returning from the hunt, preparing for bed. His life was, in many ways, like a theatrical performance. These rituals, with their rules of etiquette, were observed by the next king, Louis XV. They were still in place in 1774, when Louis XVI became king.

In addition to all his court obligations, Louis XVI managed to fit in much hard work. He awoke every morning at 6:00 A.M. to get an early start. Unlike most other Bourbon kings, he read all his letters himself. He spent hours in his white-and-gold library studying his ministers' proposals, and he often gave up hunting in order to write his replies. Louis disliked parties and went to bed at 11:00 P.M., an hour when the queen and many others at Versailles were just beginning their evenings of dining and card games and riotous entertainment.

Antoinette, on the other hand, had very little official work to do at the palace. She spent her days playing with her children, working at her embroidery, taking music lessons, or riding in the park. Full of high spirits, she often giggled behind her fan during solemn state occasions. She ignored distinguished courtiers in order to spend time with her young friends.

She also did away with many court ceremonies, so the great nobles began to stay away. Versailles ceased to be the center of their world. And as France's financial problems worsened, many servants were dismissed. The great building itself was neglected, with broken windows and crumbling masonry left unrepaired.

Marie-Antoinette is playing the harp in an exquisitely decorated room at Versailles.

On October 6, 1789, as the mob forced the royal family to Paris, King Louis turned to one of his officers who was staying behind. "Try to save my poor Versailles," he said. He and Marie-Antoinette were the last monarchs to live in the great palace. It is now a national museum.

Peasants

In the eighteenth century, most people in France were peasant farmers. Some owned their land, but most rented it from local landowners. These were usually noblemen, but could also be wealthy commoners or clergymen. Using the landowner's tools, livestock, and seed, peasants worked from sunrise to sunset to feed their families. After each harvest, they paid rent—often in the form of half their crop. Grain was the crop most commonly grown throughout the country, but different regions had their specialties: potatoes in the northeast; corn, or maize, in the south; apricots and melons in the fertile valley of the Loire.

Along the Loire and farther north were the more prosperous farms. The peasants' houses there were made of a variety of materials: wood, stone, or a mixture of clay and straw. They had roofs of slate or tile. Many had several rooms, overlooking a little garden and one or two fields. Furnishings were simple—a carved chest for storage, a comfortable chair by the fire, a cupboard for earthenware plates, homemade curtains at the windows.

Farms in the south were smaller. Some were barely large enough for a cow to graze on. Many of them had no barn. On the poorest plots of land, peasants lived in windowless huts with dirt floors and thatched roofs. To save firewood in the winter, they sometimes shared their tiny houses with their sheep or goats.

Peasant life centered around the family, and the father was, by tradition, its unquestioned head. In the words of one eighteenth-century writer, a wife should view her husband as "her leader, guide, [and] master." She should obey him, "not as a slave but as a daughter." In reality, however, women exercised much unofficial power. They worked in the fields with their husbands. Often they made extra money by spinning and weaving cloth by the fireside at night. But a woman's most important role was to rear her children and educate them in the Catholic faith. Children in a peasant family usually went to school only in the winter, and girls attended far less than boys. For most of the year, all young people were kept busy doing chores on the farm.

Work followed the cycle of the seasons. In October the fields were plowed and planted with grain. Grapes and other fruits were picked then, too. In June the peasants made hay, and August was harvest time. Then the process began again.

Religion was the other main focus of rural life. Most farms were clustered around a nearby village, and in each was an old stone church. It was the heart of the community. Many peasants walked to mass there every Sunday. Families held christenings, weddings, funerals—all the important ceremonies of their lives—in its cool interior. On Easter and Christmas, farmers and their children dressed in their best clothes and marched in religious processions that had not changed in hundreds of years. And like their ancestors before them, when they died the peasants would be buried in the same quiet churchyard.

Peasants, the majority of the people, lived by tradition. They were the last to join the Revolution. But when they did, French life changed forever.

Clothes

In the time of Louis XVI, a person's place in society was quickly revealed by the clothes he or she wore. There was a dramatic difference between rich and poor. Wealthy nobles bought the latest fashions from Paris. And if they were rich enough to live at Versailles, they needed luxurious outfits for many occasions, from horseback rides in the park to balls in the Hall of Mirrors.

At court nobles tried hard to have perfect manners, perfect posture, and a sharp wit. Their clothes were an important part of their image. Men and women of all ages had their hair curled and powdered white. Men wore hats draped with feathers, satin coats trimmed with lace, knee breeches (*culottes*), silk stockings, and shoes with jeweled buckles. Nobles of the sword carried their ornate weapons at their waists. The most important celebrations, such as the king's wedding and coronation, called for suits of real gold and silver cloth.

Princesses, duchesses, countesses, and other noblewomen wore dresses with stiff hoops, called *panniers*, that expanded their skirts on each side. The gowns were made of rich silks and velvets, often embroidered with flowers. Marie-Antoinette's dressmaker introduced strange new colors, such as a yellow called the "queen's hair," or a brownish shade known as "stomach of the flea." During Antoinette's reign, too, hairstyles had themes. In addition to bunches of feathers, women wore actual scenes in their high

Even young noble-women sprayed their hair with a grayish powder. This is a portrait of the Princess de Lamballe, a close friend of Marie-Antoinette. Devoted to the queen, she refused to leave Paris during the Revolution and was murdered by a crowd in 1792.

hairdos: tiny models of ships at sea or replicas of their babies' nurseries. Most of all, the noblewomen loved their jewels, from the diamonds in their hair to the pearls on their dresses to the emeralds in their shoes.

The peasants' clothes were different. "All the country girls and women are without shoes or stockings; and the ploughmen at their work have neither sabots [wooden clogs] nor stockings to their feet," wrote an English traveler. Another traveler noticed people dressed in rags, looking like hungry scarecrows. This was more typical of the southern areas of France, where peasants were poorest. But even in the more fertile farming regions to the north, the peasants' clothing styles had remained the same for centuries.

They wore sturdy clogs on their feet and heavy woolen or linen garments, usually grey, blue, or green. These were made at home by the women at their cottage spinning wheels, and the garments were used until they were threadbare. Only on Sundays and holidays did French peasants dress up. Then, traditionally, men wore round hats with large brims. Women wore brightly colored skirts, and in some provinces, they wore lace headdresses that had been handed down through the generations.

Styles changed during the Revolution. Nobles and well-to-do people of the third estate, in fear for their lives, threw away the

In contrast to the fine silks worn by the wealthy, French peasants, laborers, and servants wore clothes of coarse, heavy fabric that was made to last for years.

fancy clothes of the old regime. The color white, symbol of the Bourbon dynasty, was also dangerous to wear. As the republican movement gained power, French women favored long gowns similar to those worn during the republics of ancient Greece or Rome. To show support for the Revolution, people pinned onto their clothes the red, white, and blue "cockade," a badge made with ribbons. Many men wore the red "cap of liberty." Radical workers, who wore long pants, were called sansculottes. This meant that they were "without breeches," the short knee-pants worn by the noblemen of King Louis's court.

The sansculottes were workers who hated the monarchy and fiercely criticized the aristocracy. They were especially powerful in Paris during the Reign of Terror.

Food

What was a typical dinner in eighteenth-century France? For a peasant it could be just a thick slice of black bread and cheese, with watered-down wine. For a noble it could be a ten-course feast, complete with appetizers, main dishes, side dishes, several bottles of champagne, and ice cream for dessert. Diet, like so many other aspects of life, depended on one's social class.

Bread was the staple food for most of the French. It was made from grains, such as wheat, barley, or rye. Peasants ground their grain into flour at the local mill and often baked it in long loaves, called baguettes. Peasant families also consumed whatever else they could produce on their small farms or buy at the village marketplace. So in addition to bread, they might have milk, cheese, vegetables, fruit, nuts, honey, or eggs. For the poorest peasants, meat was a luxury to be eaten only on holidays. More prosperous farmers were able to keep livestock, such as hogs. In large pots that hung in their fireplaces, the French liked to cook ham, sausages, and bacon.

Diet also varied from region to region. People who lived in Normandy raised cows for dairy products and beef. Their apple orchards supplied them with cider. Brittany was known for its herring and other fish. The Île-de-France was rich in grain. Farmers in Provence grew olives and other fruits. And from Champagne in the north to Bordeaux in the southwest, vineyards provided the people with wine. In times of good harvests, many peasants ate well. But in drought years the land could not support them.

The wealthiest of the French could buy almost anything they wanted to eat, and their meals were served on delicate, hand-painted china. They enjoyed hot chocolate and pastries for break-fast. For lunch and dinner, they chose such delicacies as shrimp, partridges stewed in wine, or roast duck with truffles. Louis XVI was known for his huge appetite. He could eat an entire roast chicken—and much, much more—at one sitting.

The wealthy and the middle class both benefited from France's trade with other countries. In Paris and other cities, shops sold chocolate from Spain and tea from China. Sugar from the West Indies was used to make new types of jams, candies, and cookies. The most popular novelty was coffee, also imported from the West Indies. Coffeehouses, paneled in dark wood and lit by crys-tal chandeliers, were popular during the reign of Louis and Antoinette. People sat at tables for hours, drinking cup after cup, reading newspapers, playing chess, and talking. "No one leaves the place without thinking he is four times wittier than when he went in," joked one writer.

Life in Paris

One young man who visited Paris during the reign of Louis XVI was amazed by his first glimpse of the city: "We saw a huge expanse of houses beneath a cloud of steam. . . . It was Paris, a big city, so big that not all of it could be seen from where we stood. . . . There are so many people that nobody knows anybody else, not even in the same neighborhood, not even in his own house."

Since the year 508 Paris had been the capital of France. It was also the largest city in the country, with a population of about 650,000—an enormous number at a time when most French towns were home to fewer than 10,000 people. Located in the fertile plain called the Paris Basin and divided in two by the river Seine, Paris was like a magnet to French people of all types.

The city attracted artisans because it was a center for luxury crafts, such as glassblowing, jewelry and furniture making, and clothing design. It attracted businessmen and bankers because it was a center for finance. Students traveled to Paris to study at the Sorbonne, France's oldest university. The *parlement* of Paris drew thousands of ambitious lawyers, who wanted to be near this powerful branch of the government.

Much of the city had a magical kind of beauty—bridges across the Seine, huge stone mansions with hidden courtyards, great statues of kings on horseback, fountains splashing in public

The streets of eighteenth-century Paris were crowded with horseback riders, carriages, and pedestrians.

squares, acres of tree-lined parks and gardens. In the time of Louis and Antoinette, many of the grandest buildings were already very old. There was the Louvre, built as a fortress in the Middle Ages, now one of the largest palaces in the world. And on the Île de la Cité ("Island of the City"), an island in the middle of the river Seine, was Notre Dame Cathedral. Begun in 1163 it was one of the most magnificent cathedrals in France, a marvel of carved stone and soaring arches.

But many of the city's oldest buildings were in poor shape. The majority of Parisians still lived and worked in medieval tenements, packed tightly into dark, narrow streets. Some were skilled artisans who belonged to guilds and lived in separate sections of the city, according to their crafts—tailors, saddlemakers, cobblers, or carpenters. Unskilled workers, many of them peasants who had come from the countryside, were the poorest. If they could find no work, they had to search through garbage piles for food or beg for their bread. Often, whole families lived in one room.

The wealthy were also flocking to Paris. During the eighteenth century there was an explosion of new building. Nobles, merchants, and bankers constructed large, elegant townhouses and filled them with the finest furniture and art. New streetlights, new pavements, whole new boulevards appeared. The city limits were stretching farther outward every year.

In addition to the separate districts for rich and poor, there were also areas of the city where different social classes lived together. Houses of four or five floors were a sort of urban "melting pot." Well-to-do families lived on the first floors in pretty, spacious apartments. Teachers or other professionals might rent the second floors. The higher the floor, the poorer the tenant, all the way up to the building's cramped little attic.

The people mingled, also, in the public life of the city. Because of its diverse population, Paris was the cultural heart of the nation. During the reign of Louis XVI, more than one-third of the French could read and write. Parisians loved the city's bookshops and libraries, where they read everything from romantic novels to the works of the Enlightenment philosophers. They joined literary societies or book clubs to discuss ideas and political events. All

Workers have gathered in this Parisian tavern to play cards, drink, and talk.

but the poorest citizens could afford to buy the latest journals that were sold in booths on the street corners.

Plays and musical entertainment, too, were available to many. The wealthy sat in the balconies, while workers bought tickets for the cheap seats in the pit. For those who never entered a theater, there were free performances in the fairgrounds and street singers in the public squares.

Paris was a rich mixture of people, activities, and ideas. It had always led the nation in the past, and it would lead France in the era of revolution.

The French

PART THREE

As the eighteenth century progressed, a growing number of the French learned to read. This helped the ideas of Enlightenment philosophers to circulate—in books, pamphlets, and letters.

Voltaire (1694–1778) was perhaps the most brilliant writer of the French Enlightenment. In essays, letters, stories, and plays, he fought passionately—and humorously—against ignorance and superstition. Here is a sampling of some of his ideas, as meaningful today as they were so long ago:

François-Marie Arouet, known as Voltaire, was one of the most influential of the Enlightenment writers. Outraged by the cruelty he saw done in the name of religion, he urged tolerance and freedom of thought.

On prejudice:

Prejudice is an opinion without judgment. Thus, all over the world, people inspire children with as many opinions as they choose to, before the children can judge.

On superstition:

The superstitious man is to the rogue [scoundrel] what the slave is to the tyrant. Further, the superstitious man is governed by the fanatic and becomes a fanatic.

On tolerance:

What is tolerance? It is the natural attribute [characteristic] of humanity. We are all formed of weakness and error: let us pardon . . . each other's folly. That is the first law of nature.

On books:

You despise books, you whose whole life is devoted to the vanities of ambition and the search for pleasure, . . . but you should realize that the whole of the known world . . . is governed by books alone.

Denis Diderot's *Encyclopedia* is often called the "bible" of the Enlightenment. He dedicated himself to examining science and society in the spirit of reason.

Denis Diderot was another great writer of the Enlightenment. His life's major work was editing the *Encyclopedia,* the seventeen volumes of which were published between 1751 and 1765. This collection of knowledge and critical thought was the best-seller of the age and did much to encourage independent thinking. Here Diderot states one of the Enlightenment's most important beliefs:

Let us then suppose the mind to be, as we say, white paper . . . without any ideas; how comes it to be furnished? Whence comes it by that vast store which the busy and boundless fancy of man has painted on it with an almost endless variety? Whence has it all the materials of reason and knowledge? To this I answer, in one word, from experience.

Jean de La Fontaine was a poet who lived during the reign of Louis XIV. He is best known for his many fables, in which animals take on human traits, such as dishonesty, jealousy, and greed. La Fontaine's fables were popular for years and are still widely read today:

The Hen Who Laid Golden Eggs

When greed attempts to win all, greed
Loses all. In support I only need
Cite the old story we've all heard
Of the man who owned a hen that used to lay
A gold egg every day.
Convinced her gizzard was a treasure-vault,
He killed and opened up the bird,
Only to find an average specimen
Of egg-producing hen.
Thus he destroyed
Through his own fault
The great bonanza he'd enjoyed.
For grabbers here's a pretty warning.
In recent years it's been a common sight
To see men ruined overnight
Who tried to make a fortune before morning.

The Frog Who Wanted to Be as Big as the Ox

A frog saw an ox: in his eyes
A huge and handsome figure.
He, who was no bigger
Than an egg from top to toe,
In envy stretched and strained in an effort to blow
Himself up to the same size.
"Just watch me closely, Sis.
Tell me, am I large enough?
Have I got there yet?" "No." More huff and puff.

Jean de La Fontaine was one of France's most popular writers during the reign of Louis XIV. In addition to his poems based on traditional fables, La Fontaine wrote stories, plays, and opera librettos.

"Well, look at me now!" Another "No."
"Then what about this?"
"You've still a long way to go."
At which the poor frog, overloaded
With wind and vanity, exploded.
The world is full of men as foolish as that. . . .

Bishop Jacques Bossuet, who lived from 1627 to 1704, was a leading figure in the Catholic church in France and served as court preacher to King Louis XIV and tutor to his son, the dauphin. Bossuet believed firmly in the divine right of kings, and his ideas helped shape the monarchy, from the proud reign of the Sun King until the tragic reign of Louis XVI. Here Bossuet explains that a king's power is second only to that of God:

The royal power is absolute. . . .Without this absolute authority the king could neither do good nor repress evil. It is necessary that his power be such that no one can hope to escape him. . . .

God is infinite, God is all. The prince [king] . . . is not regarded as a private person: he is a public personage, all the state is in him; the will of all the people is included in his. . . . What grandeur that a single man should embody so much!

Behold an immense people united in a single person; behold this holy power . . . you see the image of God in the king; and you have the idea of royal majesty. . . .

In sharp contrast to the idea of the divine right of kings is the Declaration of the Rights of Man and Citizen. It is the most important document of the French Revolution. Some of its principles are:

> *Men are born and remain free and equal in rights. . . .*
> *The aim of every political association is the preservation of the natural and inalienable rights of man; these rights are liberty, property, security, and resistance to oppression.*
>
> *The source of all sovereignty* [ruling power] *resides essentially in the nation; no group, no individual may exercise authority not emanating* [coming] *expressly therefrom.*
>
> *Liberty consists of the power to do whatever is not injurious* [harmful] *to others. . . .*
>
> *No man may be accused, arrested, or detained except in the cases determined by law. . . .*
>
> *Free communication of ideas and opinions is one of the most precious rights of man. Consequently, every citizen may speak, write, and print freely.*

Élisabeth Vigée-Lebrun, who lived from 1755 to 1842, was one of the few great female painters of her day. Beginning when she was only in her teens, she built a highly successful career as a portrait painter for the aristocracy. She became friendly with Marie-Antoinette and painted her portrait at least thirty times, including a beautiful picture of the queen with her children. Vigée-Lebrun left France because of the Revolution. She later wrote

Élisabeth Vigée-Lebrun painted this portrait of herself when young. After fleeing from the Revolution in 1789, she continued her remarkable career painting elegant portraits of royalty throughout Europe.

her memoirs, which contain verbal "sketches" of many of the famous people she knew during the old regime. With a painter's eye, she describes Marie-Antoinette:

Marie-Antoinette was tall, very statuesque and rather plump . . . superb arms, small perfectly formed hands and dainty feet. Of all the women in France she had the most majestic gait, carrying her head so high that it was possible to recognize the sovereign in the middle of a crowded room. However, this dignified demeanor [manner] did nothing to detract from her sweet and kindly aspect. . . . Her features were not at all regular; she bore the long, narrow oval face of her family. . . . Her eyes were not particularly large and a shade approaching blue. Her expression was intelligent and sweet, her nose fine and pretty, her mouth was not wide, although her lips were rather full. Her most outstanding feature, however, was the clarity of her complexion. I have never seen another glow in the same way, and glow is exactly the right word, for her skin was so transparent that it could not catch shadow. Indeed I was never satisfied with the way I painted it; no colour existed which could imitate that freshness or capture the subtle tones which were unique to this charming face. I never met another woman who could compete in this regard.

Benjamin Franklin served as the American ambassador to France from 1776 to 1785. Élisabeth Vigée-Lebrun met him in Paris and had this to say:

> I was first of all struck by his natural manners; he was dressed in grey and his unpowdered braided hair fell upon his shoulders; if it had not been for the nobility of his face, I would have taken him for a stocky farmer, such was the contrast he made with the other diplomats, who were all powdered and dressed in their finest clothes, bedecked with gold and colored sashes.
>
> No one was more fashionable, more sought after in Paris than Doctor Franklin: the crowd chased after him in parks and public places; hats, canes, and snuffboxes were designed in the Franklin style, and people thought themselves very lucky if they were invited to the same dinner party as this famous man.

The tall, red-haired marquis de Lafayette was the first French nobleman to fight for the colonies in the American Revolution. In 1777, at the age of twenty, he joined George Washington's staff as a major general. He fought in the battle of Brandywine, camped at Valley Forge with Washington's troops, and helped bring about the British defeat at Yorktown. Washington and Lafayette greatly respected each other and enjoyed a close friendship. After the

American Revolution, Lafayette visited Washington at his home in Mount Vernon, Virginia. Washington sent this note to his young friend after the visit:

> *In the moment of our separation, upon the road as I traveled, and every hour since, I have felt all that love, respect and attachment for you, with which length of years, close connection, and your merits have inspired me. I often asked myself, as our carriages separated, whether that was the last sight I ever should have of you? And though I wished to say No, my fears answered Yes.*

Lafayette replied before he sailed home to France:

> *No, my dear General, our recent separation will not be a last adieu. . . . I realize that you will never come to France . . . but I will return, again and often, under the roof of Mount Vernon. . . . Adieu, adieu, my dear General, it is with inexpressible pain that I feel that I am going to be separated from you by the Atlantic. . . .*

[In fact, the two never saw each other again.]

Arthur Young was an Englishman who traveled throughout France in the 1780s and recorded his detailed observations in a book. He paid particular attention to the backward state of French agriculture and the miserable poverty of so many peasants. Shortly before the fall of the Bastille, he made these entries in his journal:

> *Walking up a long hill, to ease my mare, I was joined by a poor woman, who complained of the times, and that it was a sad country. On my demanding her reasons, she said her husband had but a morsel of land, one cow and a poor little horse, yet he had . . . wheat and three chickens to pay as [rent] to one Seigneur [lord]; and . . . oats [and] one chicken . . . to pay to another, beside very heavy* tailles *and taxes. . . . This woman, at no great distance, might have been taken for sixty or seventy, her figure was so bent, and her face so furrowed and hardened by labor; but she said she was only twenty-eight.*
>
> *By order of the magistrates no person is allowed to buy more than two bushels of wheat at a market, to prevent monopolizing [hoarding]. . . . Being here on a market-day, I attended, and saw the wheat sold out under this regulation, with a party of dragoons [soldiers] drawn up . . . to prevent violence. The people quarrel with the bakers, asserting the prices they demand for bread are . . . [too high] . . . , and proceeding from words to scuffling, raise a riot, and then run away with bread and wheat for nothing.*

In contrast to the widespread poverty of the farming regions, the port cities of France were thriving during the reign of Louis XVI. Yet in 1787 and 1788, Arthur Young noted that even in the rich ports of Nantes and Bordeaux, the spirit of revolution was growing:

> *Nantes is inflamed [on fire] in the cause of liberty as any town in France can be; the conversations I witnessed here prove how great a change is effected in the minds of the French, nor do I believe it will be possible for the present government to last half a century longer, unless the clearest and most decided talents be at the helm.*

[Actually, the government would last for less than one year after this entry.]

Marie-Antoinette's trial, conducted by the revolutionary court set up by the Convention, lasted for two days. The sentence of death was read at 4:00 A.M., on October 16, 1793. At 4:30 A.M., on this last morning of her life, Antoinette wrote to Madame Elisabeth, Louis XVI's sister, who was imprisoned along with Antoinette's children in the Temple fortress in Paris. This tearstained letter was never delivered to Madame Elisabeth because it was stolen by revolutionaries:

> *It is to you, my sister, that I write for the last time. I have just been condemned, not to a shameful death, it is only so for criminals, but to go and rejoin your brother; innocent like him, I hope to show the same courage as he did in his last moments. I am calm, as one is when one's*

conscience reproaches one with nothing. I feel deep regret at leaving my poor children, you know I lived only for them and you, my good and fond sister, you who, through your friendship, have sacrificed everything to be with us. In what a position I leave you! . . .

May my son never forget the last words of his father, which I expressly repeat, that he shall never seek to avenge our death. . . .

I sincerely ask pardon of God for all the faults I may have committed throughout my existence. . . . I ask forgiveness from all those I know. . . . I pardon all my enemies the wrong they have done me. . . . I had friends, the thought of being separated from them for ever and their grief is one of the greatest regrets I carry with me in dying, let them know at least that I thought of them with my last moments.

Adieu, my good and fond sister, may this letter reach you, always think of me, I kiss you with my whole heart as also those poor dear children, my God! How heartrending it is to leave them for ever. . . .

Marie-Antoinette's tears also fell on these words she wrote in her prayer book:

My God, have pity on me! My eyes have no more tears to weep for you, my poor children! Adieu, adieu!
                                               —*Marie Antoinette*

Glossary

absolute monarch: A king or queen who has total power.

baguette: A long, thin loaf of bread.

bourgeoisie: The middle class, which belonged to the third estate in prerevolutionary France, and consisted largely of merchants, administrators, doctors, and lawyers.

coronation: The ceremony in which a monarch is crowned.

corvée: A tax that was paid by peasants in the form of road building and road repair.

dauphin: The male who is next in line to become king.

dauphine: The female who is next in line to become queen.

deficit: An economic condition in which there is not enough money to pay one's debts.

despot: A tyrant.

divine right: The idea that a monarch's power comes directly from God.

dynasty: A line of rulers who belong to the same family.

Enlightenment: During the 1700s, the movement of writers and philosophers that fought against ignorance, superstition, and prejudice.

estates: The three main divisions in French society before the Revolution.

etiquette: Rules and manners that govern social behavior.

guillotine: An instrument for cutting off heads that was proposed for use in the Revolution by Dr. Joseph Guillotin.

Jacobins: Revolutionaries who wanted to do away with the monarchy.

parlements: Before the Revolution, powerful courts that held trials and also voted on whether or not to "register," or make official, the king's laws.

Prussia: A powerful German state.

Radical: A person or group of people who call for extreme change; during the Revolution, the most radical political goals were held by the Jacobins and the sansculottes.

Renaissance: The period of "rebirth" in Europe during the 1400s and 1500s, in which ancient knowledge was rediscovered and many new discoveries were made.

sansculottes: French workers active in the revolutionary movement who wore long pants instead of knee breeches favored by the aristocrats; the sansculottes wanted to abolish the monarchy.

sharecropper: A farmer who works on someone else's land and pays rent in the form of a portion of his crop.

taille: A tax that was paid, mostly by peasants, to the government before the Revolution.

tithe: A tax that was paid to the Church.

For Further Reading

Alderman, Clifford Lindsay. *Liberty! Equality! Fraternity! The Story of the French Revolution*. New York: Julian Messner, 1965.

Cobb, Richard, and Colin Jones, eds. *Voices of the French Revolution*. Topsfield, MA: Salem House Publishers, 1988.

Gofen, E. Caro. *France*. New York: Marshall Cavendish, 1995.

Haslip, Joan. *Marie Antoinette*. New York: Weidenfeld & Nicholson, 1987.

Nickles, Greg. *France, the Culture*. New York: Crabtree Publishing, 2000.

The Splendors of Versailles, a Teachers' Guide Supplement. New York: Marshall Cavendish, 1994.

Stein, Conrad R. *Paris*. New York: Children's Press, 1996.

ON-LINE INFORMATION*

http://chateauversailles.fr/en/331.asp
This is an exciting "virtual" trip through the palace of Versailles, with photographs of many of the palace's finest art treasures and decorative objects.

http://www.bartleby.com/65/fr/FrenchRe.html
The site contains a brief, but well researched, synopsis of the main events of the French Revolution, beginning with a discussion of the origins of the struggle and concluding with information on Napoleon and the effects of the Revolution on France and the rest of Europe.

*Websites change from time to time. For additional on-line information, check with the media specialist at your local library.

Bibliography

Ardagh, John, with Colin Jones. *Cultural Atlas of France*. Oxfordshire, England: Andromeda Oxford Ltd., 1996.

Asquith, Annunziata. *Marie Antoinette*. New York: Taplinger Publishing, 1976.

Castelot, Andre. *Queen of France*. Trans. Denise Folliot. New York: Harper & Brothers, 1957.

Cobban, Alfred. *A History of Modern France*. New York: George Braziller, 1965.

Cole, Robert. *A Traveller's History of France*. New York: Interlink Books, 1992.

Cronin, Vincent. *Louis and Antoinette*. New York: William Morrow, 1975.

Doyle, William. *The Ancien Regime*. London: Macmillan Press, 1986.

——. *The Oxford History of the French Revolution*. Oxford: Oxford University Press, 1989.

Funck-Brentano, Frantz. *The Old Regime in France*. London: Edward Arnold & Co., 1929.

Furbank, P. N. *Diderot*. New York: Alfred A. Knopf, 1992.

Hardman, John. *Louis XVI*. New Haven & London: Yale University Press, 1993.

Haslip, Joan. *Marie Antoinette*. New York: Weidenfeld & Nicolson, 1987.

Hibbert, Christopher. *The Days of the French Revolution*. New York: William Morrow, 1980.

Jones, Colin. *The Cambridge Illustrated History of France*. Cambridge: Cambridge University Press, 1994.

Kagan, Donald, Steven Ozment, and Frank M. Turner. *The Western Heritage since 1300*. 4th ed. New York: Macmillan, 1991.

Kaplow, Jeffrey. *France on the Eve of the Revolution*. New York: John Wiley & Sons, 1971.

La Fontaine. *La Fontaine: Selected Fables*. Trans. James Michie. New York: Viking Press, 1979.

Laurent, Jacques. *France*. New York: Vilo, 1983.

Lefebvre, Georges. *The Coming of the French Revolution*. Princeton, NJ: Princeton University Press, 1947.

Lough, John. *An Introduction to Eighteenth Century France*. New York: David McKay, 1960.

Manceron, Claude. *Twilight of the Old Order*. New York: Alfred A. Knopf, 1977.

Mitford, Nancy. *Madame de Pompadour*. New York: Harper & Row, 1968.

———. *The Sun King*. New York: Harper & Row, 1966.

Roche, Daniel. *France in the Enlightenment*. Cambridge, MA: Harvard University Press, 1998.

Stewart, John Hall. *A Documentary Survey of the French Revolution*. New York: Macmillan, 1951.

Tour du Pin, Madame de la. *Memoirs of Madame de la Tour du Pin*. Trans. Felice Harcourt. London: Harvill Press, 1969.

Vigée-Lebrun, Élisabeth. *The Memoirs of Elisabeth Vigee-LeBrun*. Bloomington and Indianapolis: Indiana University Press, 1989.

Voltaire, François-Marie Arouet de. *The Portable Voltaire*. New York: Viking Press, 1949.

Webster, Nesta H. *Louis XVI and Marie Antoinette*. London: Constable and Company, Ltd., 1937.

Woodward, William E. *Lafayette*. New York: Farrar & Rinehart, 1938.

Young, Arthur. *Travels in France*. London: Cambridge University Press, 1950.

Zweig, Stefan. *Marie Antoinette*. London: Cassell and Company, Ltd., 1933.

Notes

Part One: The King, the Queen, and the Revolution

Page 11 "A little laziness and much frivolity": Castelot, *Queen of France*, p. 6.
Page 12 "He looked like some peasant": Hibbert, *The Days of the French Revolution*, p. 20.
Page 13 "Oh God, oh God, protect us": Castelot, *Queen of France*, p. 73.
Page 13 "greatest desire to make people happy": Haslip, *Marie Antoinette*, p. 58.
Page 15 "city of the rich": Mitford, *The Sun King*, p. 95.
Page 16 "mules": Young, *Travels in France*, p. xxvi.
Page 17 "protectors of French liberty": Kagan, *The Western Heritage*, p. 658.
Page 19 "We die for the people!": Haslip, *Marie Antoinette*, p. 76.
Page 22 "You see, I am so terrified": Zweig, *Marie Antoinette*, p. 102.
Page 24 "lost all sense": Haslip, *Marie Antoinette*, p. 92.
Page 24 "heading straight for disaster": Haslip, *Marie Antoinette*, p. 92.
Page 24 "featherhead": Castelot, *Queen of France*, p. 122.
Page 24 "I can only foretell great unhappiness": Castelot, *Queen of France*, p. 103.
Page 25 "Why should they hate me?": Haslip, *Marie Antoinette*, p. 150.
Page 28 "My son is dead": Haslip, *Marie Antoinette*, p. 188.
Page 29 "But this is a revolt": Zweig, *Marie Antoinette*, p. 216.
Page 30 "born and remain free and equal": Kagan, *The Western Heritage*, p. 666.
Page 31 "Death to the Austrian!": Hibbert, *The Days of the French Revolution*, p. 101.
Page 32 "shadow of royalty": Hardman, *Louis XVI*, p. 176.
Page 33 "There is no longer a King": Zweig, *Marie Antoinette*, p. 311.
Page 34 "conspiring against liberty": Hardman, *Louis XVI*, p. 226.
Page 35 "superhuman courage": Hardman, *Louis XVI*, p. 230.
Page 35 "Long live the Republic!": Hibbert, *The Days of the French Revolution*, p. 189.
Page 36 "God himself has forsaken me": Cronin, *Louis and Antoinette*, p. 377.

Part Two: Everyday Life in Revolutionary France

Page 47 "I am the State": Cole, *A Traveller's History of France*, p. 93.
Page 50 "Try to save my poor Versailles": Cronin, *Louis and Antoinette*, p. 299.
Page 52 "her leader, guide, [and] master": Roche, *France in the Enlightenment*, p. 526.
Page 52 "not as a slave but as a daughter": Roche, *France in the Enlightenment*, p. 526.
Page 54 "All the country girls and women": Doyle, *The Oxford History of the French Revolution*, p. 14.
Page 58 "No one leaves the place without": Roche, *France in the Enlightenment*, p. 628.
Page 59 "We saw a huge expanse of houses": Roche, *France in the Enlightenment*, p. 59.

Part Three: The French in Their Own Words

Page 67 "Prejudice is an opinion without judgment": Voltaire, *The Portable Voltaire*, p. 179.
Page 67 "The superstitious man is to the rogue": Voltaire, *The Portable Voltaire*, p. 205.
Page 67 "What is tolerance?": Voltaire, *The Portable Voltaire*, p. 212.

Page 67 "You despise books": Voltaire, *The Portable Voltaire*, p. 90.

Page 68 "Let us then suppose the mind to be": Furbank, *Diderot*, p. 54.

Page 69 "The Hen Who Laid Golden Eggs": La Fontaine, *La Fontaine: Selected Fables*, p.127.

Page 69 "The Frog Who Wanted to Be as Big as the Ox": La Fontaine, *La Fontaine: Selected Fables*, p. 9.

Page 70 "The royal power is absolute": Kagan, *The Western Heritage*, p. 481.

Page 71 "Men are born and remain free and equal": Stewart, *A Documentary Survey of the French Revolution*, pp. 113–115.

Page 73 "Marie Antoinette was tall, very statuesque": Vigée-Lebrun, *The Memoirs of Elisabeth Vigee-LeBrun*, p. 32.

Page 74 "I was first of all struck by his natural manners": Vigée-Lebrun, *The Memoirs of Elisabeth Vigee-LeBrun*, p. 318.

Page 75 "In the moment of our separation": Woodward, *Lafayette*, p. 153.

Page 75 "No, my dear General": Woodward, *Lafayette*, p. 153.

Page 76 "Walking up a long hill": Lough, *An Introduction to Eighteenth Century France*, p. 59.

Page 76 "By order of the magistrates": Lough, *An Introduction to Eighteenth Century France*, p. 44.

Page 77 "Nantes is inflamed [on fire] in the cause of liberty": Lough, *An Introduction to Eighteenth Century France*, p. 75.

Page 77 "It is to you, my sister, that I write": Webster, *Louis XVI and Marie Antoinette*, p. 502.

Page 78 "My God, have pity on me!": Webster, *Louis XVI and Marie Antoinette*, p. 503.

Index

Page numbers for illustrations are in boldface.